The Loony Bride and Other Short Stories

S.S. Zemke

Published by S.S. Publishing, 2024.

THE LOONY BRIDE AND OTHER SHORT STORIES

First edition. June 22, 2024.

Copyright © 2024 S.S. Zemke.

ISBN: 979-8227193292

Written by S.S. Zemke.

Table of Contents

Section 1: Crazy Stories | The Loony Bride 1

Ms. Grouchy in Paradise 5

The Day the Green-Eyed Monster Died 16

Section 2: Stories from the 1800s | Outlaw with a Rolling Pin 22

Miss Mae's Hideaway 27

Orphan Burglar 31

Section 3: Flash Fiction | The Insult Machine 36

The Mysterious Lullaby 40

Tyler's Tameless Tunnel 44

Abuela's Menudo 47

The Birthday Disguise 50

From the Minds of Mothers 53

To my writing group, Footprints, for all their wisdom and helping me put my stories together.

To my mom and husband for all their encouragement.

To Mr. B, my high school English teacher and friend for helping me with rewrites.

To the Lord, for being my best friend.

Section 1: Crazy Stories
The Loony Bride

The hospital smelled of cleaning supplies. Enough to sicken the stomach. "Allison, open your eyes." Jimmy commanded.

Allison reached her hands up in the air and slapped it as if bees were surrounding her. She'd hardly slept the past few weeks. Jimmy gently grabbed both wrists and lead Allison to the hospital bed.

"You're going to be okay. It's Jimmy." Allison relaxed her back and slowly opened her eyes. Her husband of almost seven months was holding her hand. "It's weird. Seems like you're sleep walking, but you're not. Why don't you keep your eyes open?" Jimmy said.

Allison slowly pulled her hand from his and stared down at the ground. To her, someone or something was under the bed, causing it to shake like an earthquake. She imagined a creature like Big Foot, but smaller in size. Finally, the shaking stopped.

"What is it?" Jimmy asked. He grabbed her college sweatshirt. Allison was shivering. Without responding, she laid back down on the bed.

An hour passed of silence as she peered out the window. It was dark outside on that crisp fall evening, except for the football stadium lights across the road.

It really is the end of the world. That's why it's dark outside. Allison thought.

Her husband was no longer beside her. The hospital room's door was propped open.

1

"This one is going to be hard to handle," one of the nurses laughed right outside the room. Were they talking about her?

There was a knock at the opened door.

"Hey, sweetie. How are you feeling?" Allison's mom Sandra popped her head in.

No response.

"I'll get the wheelchair. They're going to be running another test."

Allison's fever was still at 104. It would be one of many tests they had given her since being admitted to the hospital from the ER the previous day.

Allison sat in the wheelchair as her mom pushed her down the hallway. She peered outside again through the window. The darkness and the idea of doing another test caused swear words to fly out of her mouth the speed of lightening.

"Stop right now! I don't want to go." Allison hit her legs on the front of the wheelchair multiple times.

Shocked at Allison's abnormal behavior, Sandra's mouth dropped open. "Allison! You are twenty years old. Stop acting like a child!"

Once they both arrived in the testing room, Allison started screaming while the two staff members tried to hold her down. One assistant looked at the other with wide, questioning eyes. He shook his head yes. Allison blacked out.

ONE DOCTOR SAID IT was schizophrenia. Another claimed she had bipolar disorder. Dr. Frank, the one who Allison thought was her brother that morning, had an entirely different approach.

"Jimmy, do you recall anything...peculiar the last couple of days? Can you tell me what happened exactly the day you brought Allison to the ER?" The doctor asked.

Jimmy thought a moment. "Allison complained about not feeling well after a friend had left. I suspect she had a stomach bug or something like that. Her friend Sarah had come to visit. She brought over some tea to share and stayed about an hour. After she left, Allison went outside for.."

"Stop right there. Tell me more about Sarah. What does she look like?" Dr. Frank's eyes widen, and he moves uncomfortably in his chair.

"Short. Long red hair. Freckles all over her face. Over the top outfits. What does this have to do with anything?"

"That's all I need. Thanks, Jimmy." Dr. Frank flew out the door.

"What was that about?" Sandra said, sitting on a chair next to Allison's bed.

"No clue. The doctors don't understand. She's hardly slept in weeks and just needs sleep. She's acting crazy because she's exhausted.

Jimmy turned on the television. The only thing on was football. Since the door to the room was open again, he spotted someone at the corner of his eye, slapping the air like bees were around, screaming and kicking at the nurses as they tried to help. One of the nurses shut the door.

"That's weird. That person was acting just like Allison."

Sandra sighs from her corner of the room and shrugs. "I just want answers. What in the world is going on with my daughter?"

There was a knock at the door. Jimmy opened it to see Dr. Frank.

"Jimmy and Sandra, could I see you out in the hallway please?"

Once in the hall, Dr. Frank took off his glasses.

"We know what's wrong with Allison." Dr. Frank whispered. He looked around the hallway, making sure no one is around.

"You do?" Sandra's lip quivered.

"You have to keep this to yourselves, okay?" Dr. Frank put his finger to his mouth. "There's been several cases over the past few months of this. Similar symptoms to what Allison has. Our tests have found that she was given some sort of...cocktail. A type of poison that makes a person... not themselves."

"Cocktail?" Jimmy and Sandra said at the same time.

"We've had five other cases like this. So far three of the five investigations have traced this back to the woman with red hair. The one you described. The other cases are still under investigation, but I'm certain it's her."

"Wow. I would have never thought that's what it was."

Dr. Frank talked with Sandra and Jimmy a bit longer, and opened the door for them to go back into the room with Allison. A woman with a large white hat sitting in one of the chairs next to Allison met their eyes. Dr. Frank's eyes widened.

"Looks like you guys have a visitor." A nurse said from across the room.

The woman turned around and jumped up to kiss Dr. Frank. She left a huge lipstick stain on his cheek. "Hey, honey. I brought you your lunch today. You forgot it on the counter again." She was short with long red hair, freckles, and was wearing genuine fur, high heels and long fake eyelashes. She slammed the door to Allison's room behind her. "You forgot to tell me goodbye before you left, dear," the woman smiled, holding out a cup of tea for him.

Ms. Grouchy in Paradise

The yard was quiet and peaceful. "You have got to be kidding me! It needs to be hacked down with an axe." The yelling pierced the silence. Ellie perked up her ears. Her neighborhood was normally quiet, and she almost dropped the glass dish she had in her lap from lunch. Stealing to her window with the sheer white curtains, she pulled them off to the side. Peering out the window, she could see an older woman in the yard next to hers with her hands on her hips, glaring over at Ellie's yard.

"That one's a weed. Stupid girl." The woman yelled again and pointed over at Ellie's yard. No one else was in sight. Ellie's stomach started to churn. She decided to wait a little while longer before going back out into the hot sun and continuing her yard work.

Ellie slammed the dish down on the counter. It shattered, but she kept on going. She cranked the hot water on to rinse the soiled dishes that were piling up on the marble counter. Staring outside the window while she rinsed, she noticed the woman's husband out in their backyard laying down some fertilizer. He had on his sun hat and she noticed something peculiar about his face. What was it? He had bandages covering a great deal of it.

Back outside, Ellie turned on the weed eater to finish trimming the edges of the yard that were in front. She thought about her neighbors and the yelling wife. They had just moved in not even a month ago. Ellie remembered their large moving truck in the driveway.

"You do know that is a weed, right?" The old lady marched right towards Ellie, crossing over into her yard. Soon enough, she was pointing her finger right up to her face. Ellie had the urge to push the lady's hand away but instead took two large steps back.

She tried to be as kind as possible, despite the woman's tone. "I'm not finished working out here. Yes, I know that one is a weed."

"You can just get the trimmers out and hack it down." The woman's eyes flared.

Ellie took a long pause. "I don't think we've met before. I'm Ellie." She took off her right glove and offered to shake the woman's hand. The woman just stared at her and didn't shake it back.

"So you're a teacher, huh?" The woman barked.

"Why yes, I am. I teach at the academy here in town."

"Gerald told me who you are. I think if you're going to live at this house, you need to be taking better care of it. Those weeds were growing so out of hand and coming over into our yard. We tried to get a hold of you, but you were never home. It's been like this for over a month."

"I have been very busy working, but now that it's summer, I have more time now to work on it."

"I contacted your boss Gerald and told him all about the yard."

Ellie wasn't sure what to say. That would explain the surprise visit a couple days ago. He had called to ask if he could borrow something out of the garage. Right before he left, he said, "Hey, go ahead and just mow these weeds down." Ellie's husband Jimmy had told her not to touch them because it was attracting a ton of yellow jackets and he wanted to help with the yard work when he had a chance.

"Hmmm....so you know Mr. Beth?" Ellie asked.

Why would this woman call my boss? Ellie wondered. She took a few deep breaths.

"Gerald and I used to take care of Marvin. He lived a while here in this house with him, and I would cook and bring over meals."

"Mr. Beth is a great guy. Wonderful principal too." Ellie couldn't think of what else to say. It took everything within her to not lash out at this lady. She wanted to stay calm and collected. She peered over at the lady, trying not to glare.

"Marvin used to hire people to tend to his flower garden, you know."

"Yes. When we first moved in here, we noticed how beautiful the flowers were." Ellie wanted to quickly finish up the yard and get back inside, but the lady kept on talking.

"His wife Eleanor took care of the flower beds herself." The lady bent over and started picking up weeds by hand out of Ellie's yard. She peered over at the rock path near the front of the yard. "I assume you know about them being...."

Ellie nodded. Mr. Beth had told her how Marvin and Eleanor were both cremated and their ashes buried in the front yard. It had been their wish since they had loved their house so much. That was one of the areas she made sure to weed first.

"You do know they were killed, don't ya?" Ellie wasn't sure what the woman meant.

"Mr. Beth told me they both died of a heart condition." Ellie said.

The woman looked up from where she was weeding. "He told you that?" she snickered. "They were killed. And not from natural causes, if you know what I mean."

Ellie shook her head. "No. I don't know what you mean."

The woman continued to weed. Ellie waited for an explanation, but finally decided to pick up her weed eater again and continue what she had been working on.

When she finally finished the front yard, the woman stood up from the spot she was weeding.

"I'm Bernice, by the way. I need to get my casserole I made earlier in the oven. Bye, teacher." Bernice marched right back into her yard.

Ellie decided she would keep working on the yard the next day. At least the front yard was finished, as well as the side flower beds. Now all she needed to do was to mow the back yard and put up some more of those bright yellow traps with meat and juice in them to capture more yellow jackets.

Her stomach was a little upset, but not in knots the same way it had been earlier when she first heard the lady's voice. What did Bernice mean by telling her that Marvin and Eleanor had been killed and not by natural causes? Mr. Beth had told her Marvin had passed away in his rocking chair while he was sleeping. He had been battling a heart condition for quite some time. The woman's words twirled around in her brain a while until Ellie's husband Jimmy came home.

"Boy, do I have a lot to tell you about today!" Ellie hugged her husband as he dropped his dirty shoes by the front door.

"My day was good," he said. Ellie smiled. Her husband always liked to tease her.

"And how was your day, dear?" Ellie teased back. He proceeded to tell her a little about the new project from work.

"So what's going on?" He finally asked. "How was your day?"

Ellie told him about eating lunch and how she heard yelling outside. She told him about the weird conversation she had with Bernice.

"Mr. Beth said Marvin died peacefully in his sleep."

"That's what he says. But do you think this neighbor lady knows something that we don't?"

"I think if something like that went on, we would have heard it all over from people in town. This town is super small. News would have spread like wildfire. If there was an investigation, I'm sure they wouldn't have rented out his house to us so quickly."

"Unless someone were trying to cover something up."

"Your imagination is running wild. I wouldn't read too much into it. Sometimes people say things and we misunderstand them."

"I guess you're right."

Ellie started cooking dinner and just before the timer was set to go off, there was a knock at the front door. Peeking outside through the window, she could see that it was Bernice holding a bag of gourmet chocolates in one hand and African daisies in the other.

"Should I even answer it?" Ellie tried to keep her voice down as she asked her husband.

"I think you should. Maybe she's coming over to apologize and wants to give you a peace offering. Or maybe you're her next victim," he said with a snicker on his face.

Ellie trudged to the front door and opened.

"Elvis. I brought you these daisies and chocolates. I do this a lot with one of my other neighbors, bringing treats and stuff."

"Thank you, Bernice." Ellie grabbed the African daisies and chocolates from her. She decided to overlook the fact that she said her name wrong. She noticed how old and wrinkly Bernice's hands looked, which seemed to contrast her face. Ellie could probably reach out and touch the veins on her hand, and they would roll around. She thought of this because her grandmother asked her to massage her hands occasionally, and this was something that Ellie always cringed at.

Bernice turned around and stepped off the front porch. Ellie pushed the door closed behind her.

"What's up?" Jimmy asked as he turned the corner from the bathroom.

"The next-door lady gave me flowers and chocolates and called me Elvis." Ellie placed them on the counter. She was tempted to dump them in the garbage.

"See? I told you. She brought you a peace offering," Jimmy said.

"Yeah...she didn't really say much. No apology. Just handed me the stuff and walked off." Ellie waved her hand in the air.

"Well at least she stopped by. That's saying something." Jimmy grabbed a couple bowls from the cabinet and two spoons and lifted the lid to the chili simmering on the stove.

"I almost had a heart attack when I heard that lady yelling. She gives me the creeps."

The next morning Ellie quickly prepared for work and threw some bacon into a skillet to start heating up. It was one of Jimmy's favorites, but something she didn't make too often.

"It's crazy. Shawn from work just texted me. He lives only a few blocks from us and said that there's been several break-ins in the neighborhood." Jimmy announced.

"Really? Any house super close to us?" Ellie pushed the bacon around with a spatula and popped some toast into the toaster oven.

"I don't know. I'll ask him tomorrow when I go in. I have today off, so I think I'm going to run to the store and price check those security cameras I had been thinking about getting."

"I think that's a good idea. Gives me shivers just thinking about it."

Work seemed to go slow for Ellie. She kept thinking back to her conversation with Bernice out in the yard. The more she thought about it, the more she felt determined to find out the real story. If there was one. She felt compelled to ask Mrs. Carol more about Marvin and Eleanor. She had lived in this town for more than twenty years and knew just about everybody's story.

Recess finally came around. At least the kids were well behaved. She was pretty sure it was because two of her ornery students were gone for the day.

Thankfully, she noticed Mrs. Carol taking a break outside during elementary recess. This was her planning period, and occasionally she would take a stroll outside to see how the elementary teachers were doing. She was a mentor to everybody in this tiny academy and a teacher for the upper school as well.

"Ellie! How are things going in your classroom? Do you need anything?"

"They are going okay. I might ask your advice later about strategies for Trevor, but there's something else I wanted to ask you. What do you know about Marvin and Eleanor, the couple that used to live in the house I'm renting?" Ellie had told Mrs. Carol before about renting the house, and how it was for only $500 a month, which was an incredible deal for a struggling teacher, especially in this town. The house had four bedrooms, two bathrooms, and a huge back yard.

"Marvin was a neat guy. I had the privilege of going over to his house a couple times. He was a huge supporter of this school back in the day and was on the board. He would have barbeques over at his house and invite all the staff in the summer before school would start. He would spend most of the time telling me about his days playing football and the shelter he used to work at before he became a doctor. He was a very successful and well-known doctor here in Montana."

"Really? Wow. I didn't know that. I knew about the football and how he helped out at a shelter, but I didn't know that he had been a doctor."

"He was retired for many years before he passed away."

Mrs. Carol then talked a little about Eleanor and how she had been a teacher as well and how she had always had a green thumb. Ellie was just about to ask her about their deaths, but the bell rang for the students to head back inside. Ellie was anxious the rest of the day and was relieved to hear when the final bell rang for school to be let out.

At home, Jimmy told Ellie how he found a good deal on security cameras and how he had them put up right away.

"Really? I didn't even notice them when I walked through the front yard."

"It was hard to find an easy spot to put that one up. I put one up on each side of the house."

Ellie was glad to have the cameras, especially since there had been recent break-ins nearby.

About a week later, on a Friday night, Ellie decided to stay up with Jimmy to watch some old movies he had checked out from the library. He had his laptop open and the surveillance window for the security cameras. Around one o' clock in the morning, she heard annoying beeping coming from the laptop. They looked at the security camera and noticed that in the backyard, near the giant storage shed, there was movement. The beeping was coming from the detected motion on the security system. She froze.

"Jimmy! Look!" Ellie pointed to the laptop. They both watched as someone walked around to the other side of the shed where the opening would be.

"What do you think we should do?!" Ellie panicked. "What if they break into the house? Do you have the taser around?"

"It's not charged up, but I have that heavy shovel by the front door." Jimmy stood up by the bed and slipped down the front stairs to grab the shovel. Ellie didn't move from her spot. He came back to tell her he was going to head out to the back yard.

"No, don't!" Ellie tried to whisper. What if they're armed or something?"

She saw more movement on the cameras again and waved for Jimmy to come over.

This time, they could clearly see that the person was carrying a box and there were some clothes on top. She could see bandages on this person's face.

"Oh my!" Ellie held a scream back.

"What?" Jimmy asked.

"That's the neighbor lady's husband! I don't know his name, but I've seen him before working out in their yard. What's he doing?"

"Looks like he took something out of the shed. But I remember clearly locking that back up. He would have had to break into the shed somehow."

"What in the world is in there that he would want?"

"I saw a couple mowers in there and some yard stuff. Also, there are some boxes in there that I've never gone through before."

Bernice's husband seemed to be looking around and then disappeared from their yard.

"Should we call the cops?" Ellie said.

"Did you say that Bernice used to take care of Marvin?" Jimmy asked. Ellie nodded, not sure what to say next.

"They must have a key to that shed and maybe some stuff is in there that belongs to them."

"Maybe. But why would they sneak around in the middle of the night? Why not just ask us? This is our place now. And he looked awfully suspicious."

"I think your imagination is running wild again. Let's just go over there and ask them tomorrow. It's probably nothing."

"Are you kidding me? What if he didn't want to get caught? He might do something crazy."

"I'll go over there with you. They need to know that we have evidence of them trespassing, and they can't mess with us. Let's just see what they say and go from there, rather than calling the cops tonight."

"What if he pulls out a gun or something like that?"

"Like I said, I'll go with you tomorrow over there and talk to them. We can make sure we're in their front yard, where others can see."

Of course, Ellie couldn't sleep well that night. She slept not even an hour and then her alarm rang. She had forgotten to turn it off, since it was set for her to get up for work during the week. Jimmy turned over, but then fell back to sleep. She thought she might as well get up and get some chores done around the house before Jimmy forced her to face the neighbors. They were always working in their yard, so hopefully it would be easy to talk to them where others could possibly see.

After breakfast, Ellie and Jimmy grabbed their light jackets to head out the door. It was cooler, and Ellie had spotted Bernice outside the window in her front yard planting more flowers. Once they finally reached their yard, though, Bernice was nowhere in sight. Jimmy noticed their front screen door was closed, but the front door was open.

"Must have just ran inside to grab something." Jimmy said. Before Ellie could protest, he was already knocking on their front door. There was no answer.

"Come on in!" She finally heard Bernice call in a hoarse voice.

Jimmy pulled the screen door open and grabbed Ellie's hand to come in with him.

Bernice was not in the front room.

"Go ahead and have a seat on the couch, Mildred! I have to get my curlers in."

"Mildred?" Jimmy whispered. "Who's that?"

"She did call me Elvis instead of Ellie the other day. Maybe she thinks my name is Mildred now?"

"That or...she thinks we are her friend Mildred."

"Maybe we should go." Ellie stood.

"No, sit. She needs to know that we saw her husband prowling around our property. That is not okay." Jimmy whispered.

Ellie and Jimmy sat for what felt like a long time. Jimmy spied a laptop in the corner of the room and headed over to peek. He was always interested in the different types out there and saw that this particular brand was a Tandy. "Wow. This laptop is old. Someone must have restored it."

Ellie came to stand beside him.

"Jimmy. Look at this." Ellie pointed. She had lifted the lid to the laptop. Bernice had shut the door to the bathroom and Ellie figured they would hear her open it. The husband's pickup truck was not in the driveway, so she was certain they were alone.

There was a folder open on the laptop about crimes that had happened all around the United States. Most were about thieves stealing thousands of dollars. Ellie clicked through the images. A few of them showed before and after pictures of people who had been through plastic surgery. Ellie quickly clicked on the right arrow key to view the next image, since it seemed like Bernice was going to be awhile. To her horror and surprise, Ellie was the first to spot it. Two pictures were side by side. One was of Eleanor, the lady who had supposedly died of a heart condition and was buried in their front yard. Jimmy and Ellie had seen pictures of her around their house, along with many other family photos and random things that the family hadn't cleaned up before they rented it out to them. The other "after" picture was of Bernice. Ellie's eyes grew wide and her heart leaped inside her chest. It stated the name of the doctor who did the procedure was Marvin Blair. She gasped.

Ellie clicked another tab. A before and after picture of a man popped up too. It was Marvin and then a picture of Bernice's husband, and the name of a different doctor who did that procedure.

"I cannot believe this." Ellie almost fell backwards. She was just about to grab Jimmy's hand and sprint out the front door, but Bernice opened the bathroom door. Jimmy and Ellie couldn't move. Bernice looked startled when she saw both of them standing at her laptop. Her eyes turned wide and fiery, even more than when Ellie first met her in the yard.

"I thought you were Mildred, my other neighbor." Bernice fumed.

"Eleanor?" Ellie blurted.

Local Couple Missing

July 20th, 2000
Paradise County Sheriff's Office
Paradise, Montana

A local teacher from the academy, Ellie Bennett and her husband Jimmy Bennett went missing two days ago. Police are conducting an investigation. Jimmy was last seen by his neighbors across the street. He was working in his yard installing security cameras. Ellie was last seen working at the school. Anyone with information regarding the whereabouts of Ellie and Jimmy Bennett is asked to call the Paradise County Sheriff's office, Duty Officer.

The Day the Green-Eyed Monster Died

Haylie had never committed a crime before. But it was a good evening for a kidnapping. Crouching low in her spot in the woods, she peered over at the light on in the downstairs bedroom. Moira sat in the rocking chair near the window, her perfect straight blonde hair cascading down her left shoulder. She was rocking back and forth. Haylie mumbled under her breath and checked her watch. It was five minutes till eight o'clock.

Haylie pictured Moira, the southern belle in her tight jeans, black boots, and sparkly Christmas sweater. "We don't feel a need to lock our doors. At least while we're awake. It's so quiet and peaceful around our property. We've never had a problem," Haylie remembered Moira bragging to her at the employee Christmas party in her thick southern accent.

Moira rose from her chair and crossed the room. Haylie checked her watch. Eight o'clock exactly. Just on time. Haylie waited till the light went out, then adjusted her position. The only lights on were the ones on the other side of the house, in the front room. Haylie knew Moira would be joining her husband to watch a movie, and the light from the T.V. would be the only one on in the whole house soon enough. She ran through her plan one more time. She couldn't wait to get back to her apartment. Everything was set up and in its place and she could finally relax.

Haylie waited ten minutes after only the T.V. was on, then executed her plan. She slipped across the back yard, grateful no outdoor lights

16

were on. Opening the back door in one slow motion, she pulled out of her boots. She wore all black, including her gloves and socks.

Haylie opened the door to the first bedroom on the right. There wasn't even a nightlight on, so she pulled out her phone to use as a light, and shined it around the room. The nursery was decorated as if it were straight out of a magazine. Clean. Organized. Tip top shape. Just like Moira. Haylie rolled her eyes. Perfect house. Perfect husband. Perfect child. Perfect life.

She peered over at Timothy, the three-month-old baby in the crib. He wore his blue and white swaddle, lying under his mobile of stars. He was snoring. Haylie thought she heard something in the hallway, so she dashed into the open closet next to her, hiding among the blankets and baby clothes. She waited.

After a while, she packed some necessities into a nearby diaper bag to take with her. Once she thought the coast was clear, she approached the crib. Slipping her fingers underneath the baby, she lifted him, surprised he didn't awaken. She had a plan for that too, just in case.

Crawling out the window while balancing the baby and the diaper bag, she sighed once her feet reached the ground, although she was cold. She sneaked around to the other side and slid into her boots that had been left by the back door, not looking back until she reached her special spot in the woods. She knelt back down and looked at the house. Her heart raced. Someone was coming out the back door.

Her first instinct was to run, but she froze in place. It was Moira's husband. He was talking on his cell phone. Haylie sighed with relief. He hadn't noticed anything. Probably just coming out to watch the stars while he chatted. Haylie relaxed, but when she adjusted her arms a little, Timothy started to cry. A loud, piercing cry. Haylie heard the husband's voice stop mid-sentence. Since he couldn't see her, she ran as fast as she could the other direction through the woods, the way she had come. Heart thumping in her chest, she tripped a couple times on some tree roots, but was grateful for a tiny bit of light from the moon and that she was able to keep the baby in her arms.

She was close to the highway, and found her pickup where she had left it, enough off the road where no one could see it, but a spot where she could remember where it was. Throwing open the door, she thought about a car seat. She had forgotten to buy one. She flung the diaper bag to the floor and laid the baby down on the front seat, holding one hand on him as she pulled herself in. Haylie looked around. No one was in sight. Grabbing the key from her pocket, she put it into the ignition. It wouldn't start. Timothy was quiet at that moment, his blue eyes gazing up at the ceiling of the truck.

After three tries, Haylie was able to start the pickup. Shaking, she drove down the highway the twenty minutes to her two-bedroom apartment. She was glad her next door neighbor's car wasn't parked in its spot yet. She didn't need any spectators. She grabbed a blanket from the diaper bag and wrapped Timothy. Clutching him close to her chest, she looked around again to make sure nobody was around.

After they were inside, she carried Timothy to the back room and flipped on the light. "Here's your new bedroom, Timothy." She grabbed his left hand, where he wrapped his fingers around hers. She laid him in the crib and he didn't cry. She turned the light off to see if he would fall asleep, and he did within ten minutes. *Moira even has a perfect baby.* Haylie headed to the living room and sat on the couch, her thoughts haunting her. *How long could she keep this up? How many lies would she have to tell?*

Haylie's plan after lying low for a couple months was to tell people how her cousin had died and left her baby in Haylie's care. It wasn't all a lie. Her cousin did pass away three months before while traveling in Europe. But no one had to know the full story.

The first couple months Haylie went out only when needed. Since the Covid pandemic hit, she was working from home to do her research anyway. She ordered groceries online and picked things up at a drive thru.

One day while taking out the trash when Timothy was asleep, she ran into her next-door neighbor.

"Hey, Haylie," her neighbor Terri smiled.

"Hey. How have you been?" Haylie resorted to her normal small talk.

"I've been better." Terri unlocked the front door.

"Really? What's up?" Haylie wanted to get back in, to make sure Timothy was okay, but stopped to listen.

"My sister. Her son is missing. They have been looking for quite a while."

"Aww. What happened?" Haylie had heard about her sister before. They were close in age.

"It was a kidnapping. Took the baby right out of the crib." Terri stood outside, but shut the door to keep the heat in.

Haylie's stomach was queasy. She ran her hand over it. "Oh my gosh. What was the baby's name?" She tried to sound casual, although she felt like she was going to throw up all over her front porch. *Out of all the people, Moira's sister might live next door?*

"Timothy. He's only three months old. Police have been looking for him for over two months," Terri said in a sad voice.

"Wow. That's a long time. How's your sister holding up?" Haylie hoped Moira had gone insane. Maybe they had brought her to an asylum.

"Devastated. On top of that, her husband was about ready to file for divorce. They had been having problems for quite some time since her cancer diagnosis."

Haylie was about to ask more questions about the marriage and Moira's health when she heard the baby. She hoped her neighbor didn't hear the cooing.

"Wow. You'll have to tell me more about it later. I have a roast in the oven I need to get out," Haylie lied.

"Okay. See you later." Terri gave Haylie a weird look.

Haylie was just about to hop through the door when her neighbor stopped her.

"You know what's funny? I was thinking about Timothy and my sister one night and I could have sworn I heard a baby cry. It was coming from your apartment."

Haylie laughed. "Really? I forgot to tell you. I'm taking care of a baby. It's my cousin's actually."

"Wow. Really? I had no idea." she sighed as she looked down at the ground. "I thought I was going crazy. Glad to hear there was actually a baby."

Haylie smiled. "Yep. Sweet little Brandon. I hope he doesn't keep you up too late into the night. Sorry if he's a bother."

"Not at all. Oh yeah. I forgot to mention. I found out my sister knows you. I was talking about you because you both like to bake with that nasty Splenda stuff. When I told her your name, she got so excited."

"Really? What's your sister's name again?"

"Moira."

Haylie acted surprised. "Oh my goodness! Moira? That's your sister? Totally cool. Not about the bad stuff, but cool that you're related to her."

"Totally. I'll talk to you later, Hay," she said as she slipped inside and shut the door.

I had no idea Moira was having marriage and health problems. All this time I thought her life was so perfect.

Haylie's loneliness had taken a turn for the worse right before the kidnapping. A single woman of thirty-eight, she felt she lacked so much. A husband. A fancy house in the suburbs with a fenced-in backyard. Children of her own. But she realized compared to Moira, she had so much. Moira had been sick and Haylie didn't even know how long ago it started. To top it all off, her marriage was suffering. And yet despite all her pain, Moira was the one with the genuine good attitude and real friends. Haylie slumped down in a seat.

Late that evening, there was a loud urgent knock at the door. Hands shaking, Haylie opened it to see a young police officer. He asked her tons of questions. She told no lies and shared every detail about the kidnapping. They escorted her to the police car. Her neighbor watched out the window. Another officer gathered Timothy and his things. Although handcuffed, for the first time in years, Haylie felt free. The green-eyed monster had died.

Section 2: Stories from the 1800s
Outlaw with a Rolling Pin

Meade, Kansas 1892
Eva needed the money. And fast. It was her last chance to ask before she would lose everything. Peering around the tiny room where her husband John and her had dined so many evenings together, she mulled over the words in her mind she had rehearsed. *Split the gang. Rob two banks at once. Each receive an equal amount. Pay the mortgage interest and the taxes on the home John had built.*

The telegram came the week before, stating how her brothers were coming for a visit. Eva wanted to be ready. The telegram was written in a code only she could understand. *Rolling Pin. EBG.*

The day of the visit, through the window she saw Grat enter the barn with his horse and the others following close behind. Hoping none of the neighbors had seen them, she thought about the U.S. Marshall in Dodge City who was asked to keep an eye on her, ever since the brothers' escapades started two years before. Even Mrs. Miller across the street had suspicions about Eva being a part of their gang. She stood near the entrance of the secret tunnel in the dining area, waiting. Eva hadn't considered herself a criminal. Until that day.

Emmett entered the tiny room first near the stove, through the secret tunnel not even tall enough for a man to stand up straight. "What are you cookin up, sister?" He sniffed the air and plopped down in a seat, resting his elbows on the table just like he did when Mama would call the boys in for supper when they were kids. He played with his handlebar mustache this time, twisting it up at the corners.

Eva grinned and patted her youngest brother's hand. "My homemade bread. John and I just finished supper and I thought I'd serve a loaf. He's out doing what he does every night," Eva sighed, shaking her head. Ever since his mercantile went out of business, he had been out playing poker each day.

As Eva lathered butter on the bread, Bob and Grat appeared. They startled her, causing her to drop the knife to the ground.

The older brothers nodded their greeting. Without saying a word, they found their spot at the table. Eva served the bread on a dish she had received as a wedding gift. The men devoured over half the loaf in under ten minutes.

Grat finally broke the silence. "How is old John?"

Scowling, Eva replied, "As I was telling Emmett, he's out doing what he does every night." The brothers nodded their head with understanding. They knew John was becoming a regular at poker.

Eva wanted to skip the small talk. Wiping her hands on her light pink apron, she dove in. "We missed our first mortgage interest payment in January, plus we've missed paying taxes on this place the last three years."

"That no good son of a..." Bob grumbled.

"Ain't no use attacking John," Emmett interrupted. "Just hit a dry spell, I reckon. It happens." He patted his mustache again and then swirled it around his pointer fingers.

"He ain't providing for Eva and in my book, he ain't no good," Bob retorted, rising from his chair. His nostrils flared. Eva imagined smoke shooting out of his ears. It didn't surprise her.

Eva peered down at her hands. It was true that many times she had the same thoughts. She often wondered why John didn't try for a different job, rather than just gambling. It was too big of a risk. They needed the consistent income. Since their business had disappeared, she brainstormed many nights about what she could do to help. Maybe she could try and sell more dresses around town. The older women always loved her designs. But she thought it would never be enough to cover the taxes they owed. That day, she had a different idea. One she knew Bob would admire.

Changing the subject, Eva questioned her brothers' latest adventures. "What's this I heard about the Santa Fe and the armed officers?" Word spread fast in Meade. The town gossips usually had it right, but she hadn't caught the full story.

Bob grinned. She knew feeding his ego would distract him for a moment from attacking John.

Grat told the story. "Bob here could tell something was fishy right away. It was a trap. The Santa Fe at Red Rock was filled with heavily armed officers. But boy, they couldn't outsmart Bob. He noticed they left the train dark and quickly told us to let it pass by."

"We robbed the next train a few minutes later," Emmett jumped in.

"How much?" Eva asked.

"About $1800," Bob replied, sitting back down in his chair. He went to grab a pipe from his pocket, but soon stuffed it back in after Eva gave a disapproving look.

Eva didn't waste a single breath. "I have a plan, and I want to see what you boys think," she hesitated. Bob seemed distracted, probably thinking about his own plans. She hoped he would listen. Desperation washed over her like a tidal wave. "Jesse James never did anything like this before," Eva stated.

"Git on with it. What is it?" Bob finally looked her in the eyes, impatience laced in his tone.

"There's two banks in Coffeyville. My suggestion is to rob the two banks at once. In broad daylight," Eva added.

The brothers looked around the table at each other. "They would for sure recognize us. We are known around them parts," Emmett said.

"I've already thought of that. Each of you would wear disguises. I even have some in my trunk from when John did community theatre." She watched Bob for a moment and noticed more than just a spark of interest.

This time, he grabbed the pipe out of his pocket, despite Eva's comments before that she didn't want them smoking in her kitchen. Bob always smoked when he was concocting a plan. This time, Eva was too distracted to protest.

"I don't like this plan one bit," Emmett almost whispered.

"I think Eva's got something. It's true that Jesse James never pulled anything off like this." Bob scratched his beard. "Can't help but wonder if it might just work."

"But two banks at once? We'd have to split up. It sounds too dangerous to me. We couldn't protect each other," Emmett protested.

Bob waved his arm in Emmett's direction, as if to sweep his comments away in the air.

"Eva needs the money, or she'll lose her home. We'd get probably triple what we got on the Santa Fe. I'm with Bob. I think we should do it." Grat looked over at Eva. "It's risky, but I think we could do it."

Eva was relieved. Two against one. She knew there were other members of the gang that weren't kin, but they usually went along with whatever Bob said.

The men talked some more, and the date was set. It would be early October when they would head to Coffeyville, giving them more time to add to their plan and be ready. Eva folded her hands on top of the table. Her work was done. She knew she could trust Bob to carry out her idea.

The rest of summer dragged on for Eva. To keep occupied, she filled her days with baking, sewing new dresses to sell, and weeding the garden. On normal afternoons, she would have sat on the front porch shelling beans and hounding John about playing too much poker and how he should look for a real job again. But the day after the brothers left, she stopped the prodding and focused her attention on other essentials, such as counting down the days to when her plan would be executed. She didn't tell John the ideas she had about the banks. It was a secret she vowed to take to her grave.

October rolled around. It was a crisp, cool fall day and the trees were turning their lovely gold and brown. Eva rolled up her sleeves to press out the dough for a cookie recipe she had made many times. She hadn't considered herself a good cook, until she would bite into one of her cookies. Baking always helped alleviate some of her anxious thoughts. She imagined the brothers with their disguises on that day, tying their horses up to the post, ready to take action. Vigorously pressing into the dough, she flattened it with her rolling pin. It had been her faithful companion countless years, a way to wrestle with her frustrations and anxiety. Was her plan going to work? What if someone were to take a shot at her brothers?

The news of the robbery traveled fast. Eva sat on her porch that evening, rocking back and forth in the rocking chair, watching the dry leaves blow away in the breeze. John pulled up a seat next to her. He hadn't escaped yet to his normal poker playing and was busy reading. She dreamed of growing old in this home, watching their grandchildren play in the yard and laughing.

A man on horseback approached their house and stopped abruptly. Eva rose from her chair. The man talked fast. She only caught some of his words.

Robbery in Coffeyville. Townspeople surrounding bank with guns. Emmett shot twenty times. The only Dalton brother to survive.

Eva wept, guilt and distress consuming her. She hadn't considered herself a murderer. Until that day.

Miss Mae's Hideaway

The smell of fresh baked apple pies from Mae's Kitchen enticed Hattie, but she couldn't leave her hiding spot in the pantry. Her hands shook as she crouched down. Legs throbbing from standing so long, she hugged them against her chest. Robert had been spotted right outside of town on horseback. Surely, he would search every place in the small town.

Closing her eyes, Hattie wished she could fall asleep. At least then she could escape the living nightmare of being on the run. She thought about how grateful she was Mae's husband, Jeb, had created a hidden spot in the back of the pantry. The wall had a small hidden door to get to the other side. There were gaps between the floor and the door, but it kept her well-hidden, only allowing the scent of pies to drift through.

The last couple nights had worn her down. After whispering a quick prayer of thanks for safety, she heard Robert's voice. Her stomach twisted into sickening knots.

"Mae, you seen any of 'em come past your kitchen?" The all-too familiar voice pierced the silence. Would she ever be a free woman?

"Naw, none of 'em past here. All the people I see either stop on the porch to get a whiff of my pies, or come on in and git a slice. You wantin one, Robert?" Mae held up a freshly cut slice on a plate, the sun bouncing off her fair skin.

"Sure is temptin, but I got work to do. Seems another one of 'em slaves escaped. Name's Hattie. Real short gal, has wild hair. You seen anything of the likes of her, you come find me, you here? I'll be in town the rest of the afternoon. Once I find her, then that's when I'll have one of 'em pies," Robert said.

Mae nodded and picked up her broom. "I hear ya. Bye now." Mae kept sweeping till Robert disappeared. Then she slipped into the pantry and closed the curtain behind her.

"Miss Hattie?" Mae whispered. Hattie's hands were shaking and sweat beaded her forehead.

"You're safe here. He'll be in town awhile longer, so stay put. Could I get you something to eat?" Mae's voice was a fine whisper. Hattie wasn't sure she felt like eating anymore but whispered, "yes please, Miss Mae. I reckon I ought to try and eat. Haven't had anything in a couple days," Hattie said.

Mae's eyes filled with tears. How many runaways had she hidden in the back of her pantry? But this was the first one in a while who was all alone. She walked back to the kitchen and grabbed a plate. She filled it with stew, mashed potatoes, bread, and apple pie. Mae checked all the front windows to make sure no one was coming before she opened the secret opening to the back of the pantry. What was this poor woman's story?

Hattie's hair was all in tangles and her dress torn and caked with dirt. Hadn't been much time for greetings when she first arrived. Mae shook her head. She couldn't let her just sit in filth. Not under her roof. She hurried to the back room to grab Hattie a fresh change of clothes, a small washing basin, and a blanket.

"Hattie, I know it be hard to sleep, but here's ya some things to freshen up first. Try and make yourself more comfortable after you git some food in ya. Don't worry none 'bout Robert. He comes in through these parts a lot, and I can't count how many folks I've hidden back here without gettin caught."

Hattie let out a sigh of relief. She was safe with Mae.

"You ain't the first to hide here, and you ain't the last," Mae said. She handed her the basin first.

"I have another worker coming in later, to help me with lunch. They know about the secret hideaway spot. But don't worry. She's really good bout not talkin to the hideaways when there's other customers."

Hattie wondered why Miss Mae had picked this spot to hide the runaways. Her restaurant could get busy at times. What must her house be like? Maybe it was just easier to feed and take care of the runaways at her place of work.

With it being fall, the days were shorter. Crisp fall leaves decorated the ground like a canopy. Mae had suggested Hattie sneak out with her husband Jeb to the hay wagon right when it became dark. Mae had calculated, based on Robert's rounds, a good time Hattie should try and leave town. But, there was something else Mae wanted to do, just to be sure.

"I'm scared, Miss Mae. What if he catches me? I can't go back there. I just can't," Hattie put her face in her hands, the tears slipping through her fingers.

"Don't worry, Miss Hattie. I got a plan," Mae grinned. She gave Hattie a comforting pat on the forearm.

Come supper, Hattie was crouched down in the hiding place, studying some of the letters Miss Mae had given her on a paper to memorize. "Ain't no use just sitting there and hiding. You's got to focus your mind on something else while you're waiting," Mae had said. "Otherwise sadness will get the better of ya. You learn to read, then you's can study the Good Book." Hattie hadn't learned to read. Never been something she could make time for.

After the dinner rush, Mae glanced up at the clock. Robert should be coming any minute.

Robert came into the restaurant, just at the time Mae expected he would. The smell of whiskey drifted into the café. Mae's first response was to kick him out, but she found a more secluded area for him to sit and plopped two pieces of pie in front of him. One was a fresh hot apple pie, straight out of the oven. The other was one of her meat pies, with several different kinds of meats. This time, he didn't appear drunk, but still carried the scent of whiskey.

"You just sit on back and enjoy that pie, Robert. The first one is my famous meat pie," Mae said, pulling a fork out of the side pocket of her apron. She gave him a real big smile and disappeared into the kitchen.

Robert finished every last bite of the meat pie, leaning back in his chair, patting his stomach. Mae watched the clock in anticipation. It wasn't long before Robert dashed out the door to the outhouse, clutching his stomach.

Mae slid into the pantry, laughing. "Guess I got good at hiding that fish in my meat pie. Heard he don't do well when he eats fish. You got plenty of time now to hightail it out of town, Miss Hattie. You be sure to stick close to Jeb, you hear?"

Hattie crawled out of her hiding spot. She had never been shown so much kindness in all her life. She gave Mae the biggest hug, wishing she could come with her. Mae handed her a sack. "Here's a little food for your journey, and another change of clothes. One day you's not gonna have to run and hide anymore, Hattie. I think we's gonna be a free nation. You remember to come by and see me again, alright?"

Hattie nodded, clutching the bag in her hands. She stepped into the darkness under Jeb's cloak and before she ducked into the hay wagon, she gave Mae another big squeeze. "I'll never forget your kindness. You're a Godsend, Miss Mae. A true Godsend."

Orphan Burglar

N ew York City, 1854
 Papa had told me never to steal. But it had been my way of life
for three months in that strange new place. One night my brother John
and I huddled against a brick building in an alley, watching a boy
rummage through the garbage can for something to fill his stomach. He
was an orphan too; from the same ship we had sailed. John scolded me.
"I seen you wanderin' the streets today. Why didn't you go to Emma?"

John's thick Irish brogue was more apparent than ever. I could see
from the streetlamps he was glaring at me, his red hair glowing like fire.
Was it redder when he was angry or did my ten-year-old brain only
imagine it? I shivered under my shawl. It was the last possession I had
from our mother. Typhoid had taken her life on the ship over to New
York City. Sometimes I thought I could still smell her scent on the shawl.
It was my little secret, but I also carried Papa's watch with me in a hidden
pocket on my dress. We had lost him too. Listening to it tick helped me
feel close to him.

"Emma has me steal. Papa told me never to steal. I went with a boy
to find another job shining shoes. He said I can come back tomorrow
with him." My voice sounded weak. I couldn't shake the cold I had been
fighting for some time.

"We did what we could to survive, Elizabeth. Emma was the first
person to come along and offer work," John snapped as he rubbed his
hands together for warmth.

I frowned at John's comment. I hated stealing. I didn't know it at the
time, but Emma was a Madam. She hired girls as "panel thieves" for the

prostitutes, having us slip our tiny hands through concealed openings in the walls to steal a wallet or watch from a customer who wasn't paying attention.

The next day I searched for the boy who helped me find the job shining shoes. He was nowhere to be found. I would have shined shoes myself but didn't have any supplies. I trudged around looking for other work, but by mid-afternoon I didn't have any luck.

I must have passed the place where Emma worked twenty times, grumbling each time as I stared at the back door. Why couldn't John take me with him to sell newspapers instead? Finally, I dragged my feet through the back door. *Working here beats starving, I suppose.* I told myself.

"Where ya been, girl?" One of the ladies inside barked. I shrugged my shoulders. I recognized her but couldn't remember her name. In my mind I called her Polly, because she reminded me of a stout seamstress Mama had worked with back in Ireland. Polly looked in a hurry. "I got a customer coming in. Wait five minutes. You know what to do." I nodded my head. I wanted to turn and run, but the sound of John's voice in my head convinced me to stay.

If I didn't do the job, I wouldn't get paid. And if I didn't get paid, we wouldn't eat. I waited for the woman to hit the wall once to tell me it was time, then in slow motion slid my tiny hand through the camouflaged opening to her room. My wrists had several splinters in them from doing this so many times before.

This man had his watch sitting on the old wooden nightstand, where many men had kept their possessions. He was facing the other way, mumbling something. My hand was shaky, but I managed to grab the watch from the nightstand. With too much confidence, I pulled my hand back real quick. The watch tumbled to the floor and landed with a thud. I gasped, hoping the man couldn't hear me. I heard him ask Polly what the noise was. I had hoped she could come up with a good explanation.

Later, when Polly came out of the room, she found me sitting in a different hallway. "Clumsy girl. That watch could have been sold for a ton of money." Her eyes were dark and the look pierced me. "Better not happen again, or I'll have to tell the Madam." I looked down at her feet and shifted in an uncomfortable manner on my chair. She smelled of whiskey, similar to what Papa's friend used to drink.

"I'll try better next time," I managed to say.

"Good girl." The woman reached for my long red hair. "You know, if you cut this mop off, you could get a lot of money for it." She twirled a lock of my hair around her pointer finger.

I reached to touch the mangy, tangled hair. I couldn't remember the last time it had been washed. Papa had always told me how pretty it was, with the natural curls and red color. I had never thought to cut it.

Before I knew it, I was sitting on a tall, rickety old stool. Polly had led me to Emma. She held a pair of scissors in her hand. "You got pretty locks, you know?" I nodded and gave her a fake smile. I wanted to appear brave, so I held back the tears. I watched my curls fall to the ground.

Maybe this venture would make John proud of me. He disapproved of most everything I did, but I was hoping that time would make him happy with the amount I brought to him. We could even buy that blanket we saw in a store window one day. And maybe even new trousers.

At the end of the haircut, Emma handed me some money, then led me out the door. "And this... is excellent. Good work today, Elizabeth." I glanced up and saw her pointing and holding up a watch. It was Papa's. I gasped. Before I could say anything, she had shut the door.

Too shy to walk back inside and explain, I trudged back to the alley, tears forming in my eyes. I thought about how it could be natural punishment for the accident earlier and dropping the watch off the nightstand. Or maybe for even concealing Papa's watch all this time. Would Emma have believed me if I told her it was mine?

My stomach growled. I remembered I hadn't eaten yet that day. I passed a bakery, the smell of fresh baked bread tantalizing my nostrils. I didn't feel very hungry, despite my body's growing demand for it.

That night I sat by John in our normal spot in our alley, rocking back and forth, holding my knees to my chest and sobbing. He asked me what was wrong, but I couldn't tell him, afraid he would be angry. To my surprise, he wrapped his arms around me and gave me his jacket, the only one he owned. He didn't talk much about it, but stroked my hair to show he noticed that it had been cut. We sat listening to the sounds of drunk grown-ups staggering through our alleyway and talking to themselves. I prayed they would stay away.

John was the first to break the silence. "Elizabeth," John whispered. "There's a minister who started a program for orphans. Tomorrow, I'm headed across town to find out about it. Something about riding on a train and heading out west to a farm. Could be like we used to have with Mama and Papa." Hearing their names made me sob harder.

That night I thought I heard John doing his own sobbing beside me before he fell asleep.

The next morning felt like a dream. John and I were given two new sets of clothes and a warm jacket. Mine was dark blue with buttons up the front. We were fed a hot meal including pea soup and cornbread. It was the first time I had ever tasted coffee. About a week later, we were headed out west on a train. I watched out the window at the corn and wheat fields passing by and thought of Mama hanging up our laundry outside near our field back home.

At the church where we were to be claimed, I observed a woman in the front pew. She had Mama's eyes and bright red hair. She wore a shawl around her shoulders, just like Mama's too. Her husband sat beside her, a watch around his wrist. It reminded me of Papa's. Despite the sinking feeling in my stomach from the memory of the watch, I noticed their eyes were gentle and their smile kind. At the end of the meeting, the couple agreed to take us in. Not able to stop myself, I ran into the woman's arms, giving her a long, deep hug.

They led us to their two-story farmhouse, white with a new fence surrounding Quarter horses. My room faced west. I watched the sunset from my window upstairs.

Papa told me never to steal. But that night, before I climbed into my trundle bed, I stole a kiss from the bright-eyed lady with the shawl and red hair, a piece of Ireland right there with me.

Section 3: Flash Fiction
The Insult Machine

Morgan slumped back into her shabby office chair for her lunch break just as the phone rang on her desk. Her stomach churned, knowing it was coming. She had never been called to the principal's office when she was a kid, but this school year already, she had experienced it seven times.

"Morgan?" A voice hissed on the other end of the phone.

"This is Morgan," she rolled her shoulders back, since her back hurt from working out the night before. It was a way to work off stress from her job.

"This is Ms. Lindy. I think you know why I called. Come up to my office during your planning period. We need to chat." Ms. Lindy didn't wait for a response. She hung up the phone right away.

Morgan sighed. Another missed planning period she needed so bad. She was getting behind on her grading, as the stack of papers on her desk showed.

"Hey Ms. Lindy," Morgan said in her normal cheerful voice as she approached the principal's desk.

Ms. Lindy frowned. "Have a seat," she pointed with her perfect manicured nail to the chair in front of her desk. "This is the eighth instance we've had with Bo since the beginning of the year."

"I'm aware of that," Morgan looked down at the ground. She had three students in her class this year she struggled with often but was only called to the principal's office when something pertained to Bo. The

36

teacher next door thought it was because of who his parents were. They were big supporters of the school. Very wealthy and hard to please.

"Taking a child's family heirloom calls for disciplinary action. I will be taking this one to the board."

Morgan looked up at Ms. Lindy. "That's not at all what happened. Bo brought in the necklace for show and tell. He asked me to keep it in my desk till the end of the day. Said someone special gave it to him. He forgot to come get it after school. The next day when he asked for it, I looked in the same spot, and it was gone."

Ms. Lindy bit her lip and her eyes narrowed. "And was this heirloom locked up in your desk, Morgan?" Ms. Lindy picked up her hot steaming mug of tea. Morgan hoped it would burn her hand, but it didn't.

"No, it wasn't. But I..."

"Then that tells me you either took it and are lying about it, or someone else stole it right out of your desk. Either way, you are responsible. This will be brought before the board Wednesday morning. It's not just about this instance, Morgan. It's about all the trouble you've had with Bo." Ms. Lindy stood, towering over Morgan. "You don't know how to deal with him, and the board is going to hear about that as well." Ms. Lindy shooed her out just as her fiancé entered the room. He had a dozen roses soaking in a vase.

"I'm surprised anyone would want to marry the witch. She's such an insult machine," Morgan vented to her mentor teacher, Mrs. Ellis the next day at lunch.

"She's marrying him for the money, you know. He's marrying her because his parents wished for it. Mommy's boy, I hear."

On a normal day, Morgan didn't like to hear gossip. But her mood was low and anything negative against Ms. Lindy at that moment made her feel better.

"She also has an illegitimate child. She had an affair on her first husband and birthed a child with the guy. Tried to keep it a secret. But everyone knows now," Mrs. Ellis crunched the last of her chips from the bag and downed her chocolate milk.

Morgan was distracted. "I have an idea. I saw a necklace at the mall that looks like the one that was lost. I'll simply replace it and tell Ms. Lindy it was in that drawer all along."

"You could try, I guess. She'll probably find something else to complain about or just say you stole and it and want to give it back to clear your name. Who knows," Mrs. Ellis shrugged.

"It's worth a shot. I don't want to get fired or not have my contract renewed for next year. I need the income and I want to prove to myself I can withstand this jerk." Morgan stood, determined to find a replacement necklace after school. But what would the board say about all the times she struggled with Bo? The random outbursts he would have, the low grades he earned, her not being able to deal with his parents?

She was able to purchase the necklace, but when she gave it to Ms. Lindy in her office, she tossed it into the garbage can. "It's a fake, Morgan. Don't think you can fool me." The phone rang and Ms. Lindy answered it, said a few swear words, then walked out the door, leaving Morgan alone in the chair.

Feeling defeated, Morgan buried her head in her hands, then something caught her eye. A paper on Ms. Lindy's desk was peeking out from underneath a pile of papers. It had Bo's name at the top and was signed: Love, Mom. She knew it was Ms. Lindy's handwriting since she had written out so many negative evaluations for her over the past four months.

She grabbed the paper and the necklace that had been missing fell to the ground. *No wonder Ms. Lindy knew the other necklace had been a fake.* Shoving the paper and the necklace into her pocket, Morgan slipped out the door.

She hoped the board would understand Ms. Lindy was being hard on her with Bo because he wasn't just any other student. He was the principal's child. Bo had taken the necklace out of Morgan's desk to make her look bad. And Ms. Lindy knew it. Morgan walked out with the evidence, chin up, and headed to the board meeting.

The Mysterious Lullaby

"I'm telling you, I heard a piano in the middle of the night. It was coming from the woods," Addie persisted, grabbing the last tapioca out of the fridge.

"Michelle was right next to you. Did she hear it too?" Jethro stuffed the last bit of pizza into his mouth.

"She sleeps like a rock. I was already awake because I was uncomfortable. It's not easy sleeping out on that balcony, even with that air up mattress." Addie massaged her back.

"It was probably just Grandma Rebecca playing her music on the stereo."

"Grandma doesn't listen to piano music. Why would she play it in the middle of the night, out in the woods?"

Jethro shoved the pizza box into the trashcan. "Whatever, Ad. You were probably dreaming. I gotta help Grandpa with the cattle. See ya." Jethro waved, crossing the kitchen towards the back door.

Mad no one believed her and because she was asked to hang out in the lighthouse room with Great Granny, Addie dragged her feet down the long hallway to the other side of the mansion. Mom was untangling Grandma Madison's gray hair with a comb. Addie threw the tapioca and the plastic spoon onto the bed then plopped down on the carpet.

"Thanks, Addie. Could you grab Granny's baby doll? She's been asking for it."

Grumbling under her breath, Addie yanked the baby doll off the floor and threw it in their direction.

"Don't you hurt that baby!" Grandma Madison screamed. Addie jumped out of her skin.

"Remember what we talked about, Addie," Mom said.

Addie rolled her eyes. "Yeah yeah. She thinks the dumb doll is real. I wish I could just play upstairs right now, "Addie mumbled under her breath so her mom couldn't hear.

It had been three months since Grandma Rebecca had hired mom to take care of Granny Madison during the day. A nurse came out to help at nights. On a property with 2,000 acres, six huge bedrooms, an upstairs, a pool, a game room, and two large living rooms, Addie had much to explore for an eight-year-old.

That next weekend, Addie's cousin Michelle came over again to spend time at the mansion. "Hey, we should sleep out on the balcony again tonight and look out at the stars. That was fun last time."

She thought up an excuse. "I think it would be fun to sleep in the western room tonight. It would be easier to sneak out and spy on the grownups."

"Is it because of the music you heard last time?" Not even Michelle had believed her. "Come on. Face your fears," she added.

That night, dragging the mattress outside to the balcony, Addie shivered, then grabbed an extra quilt from the flower-themed room. Drifting off to sleep, Addie felt better about sleeping outside since Michelle had distracted her with stargazing and popcorn. She was about to fall into a deep sleep when she heard the same music again.

Opening her eyes, Addie saw her cousin sitting up, looking out in the direction of the woods.

"So I'm not crazy," Addie whispers.

"Let's go back inside and tell somebody," Michelle whispers back.

"By the time they get out here, the music will probably stop." Addie gasped. "I have an idea. Let's go down to the woods and see if we can find where the music is coming from."

"You're crazy." Michelle shook her head. "It's dark out."

"I have a good flashlight. Come on." They tiptoed down the back staircase, heading down the long hallway and into the pool room. At night, Grandma Madison kept the dim lights on. Addie loved when the lights would reflect off the water, along with the blue tiles aligning the hot tub.

She pushed open the back door to the pool room. "At least it looks clear out," Addie whispers, looking up at the sky. She laughs. "It's funny how I was the only scared one at first, but now we both are."

"Are you scared right now?" Michelle asked.

"Very scared. But I've never been outside in the woods at night. I think it could also be fun."

"Uh...sure." Michelle mumbled. They entangled their arms together and walked west, the piano music still playing. Addie stumbled on a couple rocks along the way. The music grew louder. This time, Addie recognized the tune as *Canon in D* by Pachelbel, a song her piano teacher had performed for her. It was one of her favorites.

Once the girls maneuvered around another cluster of trees and up over a clump of dirt, their eyes rested on a beautiful grand piano. One single candle sat on top, a woman meticulously playing at the keys. Another woman with long, black hair and a skinny, long face looked their direction.

"You shouldn't be here at this late hour, girls," the woman said. She stood and walked towards them, reaching her hand out. The girls screamed at the stranger, unlocked arms, and ran back towards the mansion. Grandma Rebecca was just getting into the pool for a midnight swim, shocked to see the girls burst through the door. The girls proceeded to tell her what they saw.

Grandma laughed. "Didn't I tell you? Granny Madison goes out to play piano sometimes at night. We bought a used piano to wheel out there that we keep in a shed. Since she has trouble sleeping, we thought it could relax her. She may have dementia, but she still remembers how to play. The other lady you saw was the new nurse."

Addie looked down, ashamed. Many days she had seen Granny Madison as nothing but a crazy old woman with a temper. She thought about the song she heard out in the woods and how beautiful it was. There was so much she didn't know about Granny. Addie vowed that the next morning she would sit and eat tapioca with her and play her the new music she learned on the piano.

Tyler's Tameless Tunnel

A Short Story for Kids

Tyler had a terrific, terrifying, totally transforming idea. As new president for a club, it was his job to pick the adventures.

He gave his friends an assignment. "Each of you bring the biggest cardboard boxes you can find. We're going to make the world's biggest tunnel here in my backyard. We'll wrap it, we'll tape it, and we'll celebrate it," Tyler said.

The next day, the yard was covered in boxes. It was time to raid the giant craft box. It had everything from grape scented markers to glitter. The club worked together to connect the boxes, then decorated.

At the end, Tyler gave each of his friends a high five, promising to play in it the next morning.

Tyler hopped into bed that evening, thinking about all the fun times they would have. But at night, the rain came. Pitter Patter. Drip drop. The wind blew and blew. Tyler slept through it all.

The next morning at breakfast, he peeked out the window to gaze at the beautiful tunnel. Tyler yelped when he opened the shades.

"The tunnel! It's destroyed." Tyler hung his head. What was he going to do? He would be fired as the president of the club for sure. He just knew it.

His friends would arrive in a few hours to play. He paced back and forth and pondered.

Maybe paint would do the trick to patch it up. He grabbed a bucket of paint from the garage. After painting the first box, it looked like a big, giant blob of blue goop.

Tyler used more duct tape to patch up holes, but it only made it worse.

Tyler hurried to the back of the grocery store to grab more boxes, but they were out. Tears came with each step as he dragged himself home. There was nothing left to do but count down the minutes.

Once his friends arrived, they stopped in their tracks. "What happened?" A boy named Cash cried. "All our hard work is ruined!" Tyler put his face in his hands. "I'm so sorry. I didn't know there was going to be a storm." Cash's face was like fire. He was always the hardest of the group to please. Tyler braced himself to be fired as president. But then his best friend Max jumped in.

"It's okay, Tyler. It was an accident," Max said. Max climbed into the section of the tunnel that had been painted blue and waved his arm for others to join. A few followed him. Tyler watched, his shoulders slumped. He waited and waited, but his friends still didn't come out. What were they doing?

Finally, Cash's head popped out, his anger dissolved. "Tyler! You did an amazing job. Come in and join us." Tyler stared, puzzled. What was Cash talking about? Their masterpiece had been ruined and all he could say was 'he did a good job?'

Tyler slowly crawled through the entrance. Suddenly, everything transformed. He blinked his eyes. It was no longer the tunnel that had been ruined by the storm. It was an outdoor wonderland with tons of unique animals. He followed his friends around.

"How did you know these were all my favorite animals?" Cash said. But Tyler had never heard of any of them. He discovered a tasseled wobbegong, or a carpet shark by the shore. In the woods, they watched a mountain chicken, which was actually a type of frog. He observed an aye-aye, a lemur from Madagascar. Each name made Tyler laugh when his friends said them out loud.

As everyone explored, Max came up beside him. "What do you think, Tyler?"

"I can't believe it. I thought I was going to lose my place as president. How did this happen to our tunnel?"

Max smiled. "I saw how it was destroyed early this morning. I thought you might need help." Max suddenly had a terrific, terrifying, totally transforming idea. "I kind of want a different adventure. Let's make this Cash's tunnel. And we can make a new magic one. It'll be fun. We'll wrap it, we'll tape it, then we'll celebrate it."

Tyler gave Max a fist bump. They were the best team around.

Abuela's Menudo

Short Story for Kids

Lucia couldn't wait to hear what Abuela had planned for them to make together the next day. She called into the kitchen. "Abuela! What will we be cooking tomorrow?"

"We will be making my famous menudo," Abuela said.

Lucia frowned. Her brother had told her about the menudo. He had to run to the back room and hide his nose under a pillow. The idea of eating a soup with tripe, which was cow's stomach, made her own stomach churn.

That night, Lucia couldn't sleep. How could she tell Abuela she didn't want to make menudo without hurting her feelings? She thought of all the dishes she had made on their visits. Arroz con pollo, chili rellenos, and her favorite-tres leches, a moist cake made with three kinds of milk. Why couldn't they make one of those again?

The next afternoon, Lucia trudged into the kitchen and plopped down at the table. She mumbled to herself, crossing her arms and waited for Abuela.

"Let's get started!" Abuela said. She danced to the fridge and grabbed the honeycomb tripe, rinsed it off, and trimmed the fat. Lucia helped her cut it into small cubes while they waited for a pot of water to boil.

"You know what is so special about this recipe, mi nieta?" Abuela always called her this, which was Spanish for 'my granddaughter.' "When I moved from my home on the west coast to the Midwest, I felt so alone. I was the only Latina at my new school, and it was not easy to fit in."

Lucia's frown turned into a half smile. Abuela always sensed what Lucia was going through. She thought about her own new school and how she didn't feel like she fit in either. People viewed her as just a shy Latina. "So how did this recipe help you, Abuela?"

"Well, one day I came home from school and my Papa had made this menudo. I ate the soup with him, and we laughed about cow stomach. He cheered me up after a bad day." Abuela gently stroked Lucia's cheek. "Remember, Lucia. Sometimes there is more to a recipe than just the ingredients."

The water boiled, and Abuela dropped the chunks of tripe into the water." I want to share my story with you, Lucia. It's a part of who you are too."

Abuela mixed up some hot chocolate, and they sat in the living room while the tripe boiled. Lucia smiled as she stared at one of the pictures. Her and Abuela had aprons on in the kitchen, holding wooden spoons. She could remember taking that picture six years before, when she was only five.

"When my family moved, it was my last year of high school. I was sad to leave. I'm glad we did though, because I wouldn't have met your grandfather and be here with you right now, making my favorite foods," Abuela said.

"The first day at my new school, I came in with my hair and make-up done, and each person sitting at their desk stared. I was the only one who liked dressing up."

Lucia sipped on her hot chocolate and imagined Abuela making her grand entrance into the school. At least she had been noticed. Lucia felt invisible to her new classmates most days.

"It was hard for me to make friends at first. I wanted so much to fit in, but my Papa taught me not to be afraid of who I was- an outspoken, west coast girl at heart. With our family being Latina, I realized it was important to also be proud of my heritage and who I was. Being different was something to be celebrated, not something to be hidden."

Lucia thought about the girls she sat near in class. Could it be possible the kids at her school would learn to love her for who she was too?

After the tripe had boiled for a while, Abuela showed Lucia how to make the rest of the recipe using potatoes, beef stock and several spices. Lucia loved mixing the pot of soup and watching her grandmother do a jig around the kitchen. Her brother had been wrong. Menudo was a dish she was excited to try.

Abuela taught her how to make the guajillo sauce and opened a can of hominy. Although Lucia had never met her great grandfather, she felt connected to him through this recipe. All the comfort he had given her grandmother, somehow spilled over into Lucia's heart. Lucia breathed in the aroma once again. Tasting it was even better. Then she had an idea.

"Abuela? Do you think I could share this recipe with my class? We're doing a social studies unit, and we can bring in food from different cultures. I want to tell them about my great grandfather and your story."

Abuela beamed. "It's *our* story, Lucia. And nothing would make me happier."

The Birthday Disguise

Short Story for Kids

One hot July day, Timothy and Ben's parents were decorating for a birthday party outside.

"It's too hot. Wanna play hide-and-seek in the house?" Ben asked Timothy.

Timothy wasn't sure. They had played the game so many times, he was running out of hiding spots. But since it was Ben's eighth birthday, Timothy agreed.

He was at twenty when he heard Ben scream. "Help!"

He ran around the corner to the basement door. Timothy opened it and noticed Ben's head was stuck in the railing at the bottom of the stairs.

"A friend said he could fit through the railing on his stairs, and I wanted to try, but now I'm stuck!" Ben cried.

Timothy told Ben to move his legs and wiggle out. But that didn't work. He tried pushing him out, but that didn't work either. He even tried tickling him, but he wouldn't budge.

Suddenly, Timothy had an idea.

"I'll be back," Timothy said as he walked up the stairs. "Wait here," he laughed.

Timothy peeked outside and noticed the guests arriving. He was so excited and ran up the stairs to Ben's room and tried on clothes, deciding to wear Ben's white pants and striped shirt. As brothers, they looked a lot alike, except Ben was taller and his hair was usually gelled. Timothy found a couple pairs of socks to make himself look taller in Ben's shoes.

He grabbed blue-rimmed sunglasses. Using the hair gel, he made his hair stick up like Ben's. With his disguise, surely nobody would notice. For once, he could pretend to be who he always wanted to be.

Timothy went outside. One of Ben's friends Conner waved.

"Happy Birthday, Ben!" Conner handed Timothy a nicely wrapped package. He followed him to the gift table.

His friends had set up a game of baseball, and told him to join. Timothy's stomach swirled. He was terrible at baseball and couldn't hit no matter how many times he tried. The game ended up a disaster, with not even one point for his team.

When it was time for cake, Timothy panicked. There were strawberries on it and he would break out in hives if he ate them. The guests would surely know something was wrong if he didn't eat it. With the friends gathered around, they sang happy birthday and Timothy blew out the candles.

His mom came outside from preparing more food in the kitchen. "Tim? Where is your brother and why are you wearing his clothes?" Timothy gulped. He should have known. Of course his mother would know it was him.

"I...uhh..." Timothy was sweating. What could he say? He thought up several lies. He could say Ben was sick and that he made him wear the outfit. Or he could say Ben was getting ready and would be there in a few minutes.

Timothy turned bright red and hung his head. "Ben is stuck," he said.

"What? Where?" His mom put her hands on her hips.

Timothy knew the truth was the best choice, although he didn't want to tell it. "He's in the basement. We were playing a game and he wanted to see if he could fit through the rails while he waited. He's there now and needs help."

With assistance from Mom and Dad, they were able to pull Ben out of the railing. Who knew lathering butter on would help him slide out?

The next hide-and-seek game with his brother after that crazy day revealed something to Timothy. He decided to hide in his parent's room. When Ben came to find him, he started to cry. Ben asked what was wrong.

"You always win at every game. You're so good at baseball, you get perfect grades, and everybody notices you. That's why I dressed up like you at the party. I wanted to be you, not me for once."

Ben took Timothy by the hand and led him to their mom and dad's mirror in their bathroom. "Look, Tim." Timothy studied the mirror. Taped to it, were three of the poems he had written the year before. He thought they had gone in the trash. "You are talented in so many ways. People notice and sometimes you don't even know. Don't ever wish you were someone else. We like you the way you are."

Ben gave Timothy a bear hug. "I got some ideas for *your* next birthday party, by the way," Ben said. "Wanna play hide-and-seek? We have plenty of butter in case something happens."

From the Minds of Mothers

P *regnant.* Two empty pregnancy test packages were strewn over the bathroom counter. I sat on the floor leaning against the white wall, clutching my fists full of hair. Wringing my hands, I glanced at the time on my cell phone, realizing it was Peter's usual time to get home from work. Curling my legs up, I buried my head between my knees, waiting for the sudden wave of nausea to pass.

Five minutes later there was a tap at the door. "Please hurry. I gotta go really bad," my husband Peter complained.

"Just give me a minute," I croaked. Tossing the pregnancy tests into a plastic grocery bag, I shoved it underneath the bathroom sink behind some cleaning chemicals.

Standing over the sink, I wasn't sure if I was nauseous because of morning sickness or from nerves. I hadn't expected to get pregnant that soon. There was no way we could afford the medical bills and other expenses.

I opened the door and trudged to the kitchen. "What's for dinner?" Peter walked in just as I was filling my water bottle. I stopped and stared at him.

"Really? Do I have to make dinner for you every night? Are you not even capable of getting yourself something?" I stomped back into the bathroom to get ready for work. Marsha had asked if I could come into the restaurant for a couple hours that night, since they were short-handed.

Peter stood in the doorway to the bathroom, his arms crossed. He was wearing his lumberjack-looking shirt again with a red plaid jacket and jeans. His beard hadn't been trimmed in months. "You don't have to be rude. I just asked you a simple question," he grumbled.

I continued to apply my mascara, hoping he would go away but he continued staring at me, waiting for an explanation.

"I have to get to work. Someone at the restaurant went home sick and I was asked if I could pick up extra hours. We need the money," I growl.

"You are always worried about money, aren't you? Why don't you just give it a break?" Peter rolled his eyes.

"Why don't you work more hours?

"Why? We have enough to get by. I'm already working overtime. You're the one who wanted to live here. The rent on this place is way too expensive."

"If it was up to you, we'd be in that crappy trailer next to a meth lab."

"No matter where we live, you always find something wrong." I knew Peter's blood pressure was rising. His face turned red, his eyes bulged out.

Applying deodorant, I pushed him off to the side, making my way to the bedroom to find my comfortable work shoes. I tied my shoelaces as fast as I could, grabbed my black sweater, keys, and raced out the door.

The crisp air blew loose strands of brown hair into my face. I didn't have time to curl it, so I just tossed it up into a messy bun. I fiddled with the keys, still shaking from the news that I'm pregnant. How was I going to tell Peter?

The car wouldn't start. I stopped myself from heading back in and asking Peter for help. I walked, remembering it was only 5 blocks anyways. The small town of Spring Mountain, Montana was quiet as I trudged through the sleepy streets. I counted the pumpkins in people's yards, trying to distract my mind. At least this part of town was sleepy at that moment. During tourist season, each street was bustling with visitors, touring the shops or during the winter season, on their way to the local ski resort.

Finally reaching the restaurant, I spied Missy standing behind the cash register, handing an older gentleman back his change. My heart sank. It was going to be a long night working with that crabby coworker.

I wore many hats at the restaurant, but tonight I was a waitress. During the dinner rush, the place was full of customers ordering the special-Marsha's pot roast, garlic mashed potatoes, and roasted asparagus with a side of her secret sauce. It was something I had to recite over and over again.

"What can I get for you this evening?" I said in my cheerful voice, although I was feeling the exact opposite.

"I'm just having dessert tonight," the young man said. "Peach pie with whipped cream, of course." I nodded my head, telling him it was a good choice. There was a familiar plaid shirt at the corner of my eye. Thankful I had just taken an order, on my way to the kitchen, I ducked behind a wooden beam, hoping Peter wouldn't see me. Too late.

"Just what is your problem this evening, Chloe? I can't figure you out. Why did you walk and not take the car?"

"I'm in a hurry. Let me through," I hissed. "And what are you doing here?"

"Thought I would get some pot roast, since there's nothing in the fridge." Peter rubbed it in. His eyes smiled.

"There's sandwich stuff, you big baby," I kept my voice quiet as others were eating at the booths near us.

"I won't let you get back to work till you tell me what's bothering you. I know you. There's something going on."

Annoyed, I moved to step around him, but he blocked the way.

"Okay! I'm pregnant, alright? That's what's going on. There. You happy?" I yelled loud enough that every person in the restaurant looked our way.

Missy

This is just not working out. Clicking out of my text messages, I slammed the phone on one of the new tables Marsha had just bought the day before for the restaurant. Another breakup. This had been what? my fourth relationship since high school. The breakups were always about the same thing. The secret I had been carrying around for years, the baggage I brought into every relationship, no matter how much I tried to hide it.

"You doing okay?" One of my drinking buddies, Candace, walked into the restaurant. I had texted her earlier that day, letting her know what time my lunch break was.

"Do I look like I'm doing okay?" I sneered down at my phone.

"You want to head downtown to the brewery after you get off? I hear it's trivia night," Candace said, her voice hopeful.

"No, I don't. Just leave me alone." I closed my eyes, wishing she would walk away.

"You're the one that asked me to come here. I know you're always this grouchy, but did something happen today I don't know about?" It was the first time I'd ever seen Candace look concerned.

"I hate this day. I always seem to be the one who gets the rude customers who don't care about anything but looking good for their friends. They come into the restaurant or whatever this place is and order a bunch of stuff and get mad if you do one little thing wrong. It's never ending." I tried to keep the subject off the breakup, not wanting to talk about it yet. Or maybe ever. Besides, Candice was only my friend because she liked to go out drinking with me. We didn't talk about the deep stuff very often, and that was fine with me.

"And ugghhh! That woman I work with. I found out her name is Chloe. I've worked with her how long? and just found out her name. They don't make us wear name tags and I honestly didn't really care to ask. All she ever talks about is her pregnancy and babies."

"You've talked about her before." Candace started to bite her nails. "You guys used to get along."

"I was so close to just telling her I really didn't care. I don't give a hoot that she's planning on having a midwife deliver her baby. Or that she's having random cravings for cinnamon bread. And her outfits. I mean come on. Are clothes that limited in town that all she can ever wear are the same stupid shirts over and over? How lame is that?"

"Is Chloe around here?" Candace asked, spitting her fingernails out to the side of the table.

I cringed. "No. She went home. And even if she was here, I wouldn't care if she heard me. What a loser."

"Wow. She really gets under your skin, doesn't she?" Candace pressed.

I rolled my eyes. "Obviously. She's also one of those people who try and shove their beliefs down your throat. Prayer this and prayer that. If I hear her talk about it one more time, I'm going to tell her off."

Candace laughed. "Why does it surprise me that you haven't already done that?"

I ignored her comment and stared at the contents on my plate. For some reason the turkey sandwich on rye with extra mayo didn't sound good anymore.

I saw Candace shake her head as she studied a menu. Without even saying goodbye, I headed to the back room for a bag to store my lunch in for later. I was glad my shift was only a couple more hours. My head was pounding, and my stomach held sharp pains. I dragged through the rest of my shift, gritting my teeth and clenching my fists. I even scared one of the customers off with my impatience as I waited for them to order. It wasn't my fault they were so indecisive.

At the end of my shift, I walked home grumbling under my breath. Snow was coming down and the wind was blowing hard. I didn't have the right clothing, thinking there was going to be at least a month more of fall. I only had my light gray jacket and a baseball cap. Shielding my face with my hands, I pressed against the cold. My long, dark hair whipped across the side of my face and I thought my hat would blow away.

Slamming my apartment door behind me, I found my favorite fuzzy blanket and slipped into the cold bed. With my nightstand beside me, I reached over and pulled out an old journal from fourteen years ago. A picture fell out from the first page. I swallowed hard.

Laura Beth, 2 days old. The back said. The sweet baby was wrapped in a pink and white blanket, a little bow in her dark, curly hair. It had been the first time I caught her with her eyes open long enough to take a good picture. A smile tickled her face. My head still pounding, I laid the picture beside me, buried my head under the blanket, and struggled to fall asleep.

About the Author

S.S. Zemke resides in the northwest with her mountain man and two kids. A teacher for children, she enjoys writing stories for both kids and adults. Her works include short stories, Christian fiction, historical fiction, and picture books.

Read more at https://sszemke.blogspot.com/.